Flower Girl Dreams

Also by
Debbie Dadey

MERMAID TALES

Coming Soon

Mermaid Tales

★ Debbie Dadey ★

Illustrated by
Tatevik Avakyan

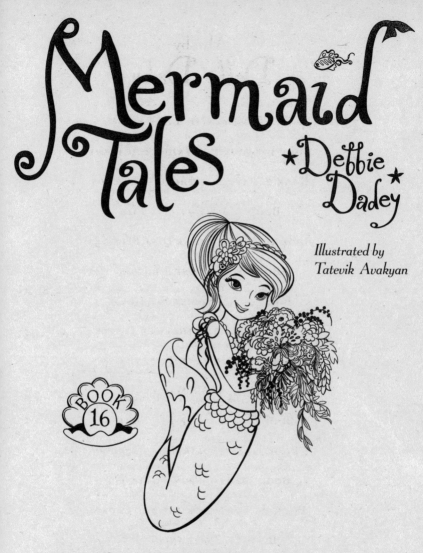

BOOK
16

Flower Girl Dreams

ALADDIN

NEW YORK   LONDON   TORONTO   SYDNEY   NEW DELHI

This book is a work of fiction. Any references to historical events, real people, or real places are used fictitiously. Other names, characters, places, and events are products of the author's imagination, and any resemblance to actual events or places or persons, living or dead, is entirely coincidental.

ALADDIN

An imprint of Simon & Schuster Children's Publishing Division

1230 Avenue of the Americas, New York, New York 10020

This Aladdin paperback edition January 2017

Text copyright © 2017 by Debbie Dadey

Illustrations copyright © 2017 by Tatevik Avakyan

Also available in an Aladdin hardcover edition.

All rights reserved, including the right of reproduction in whole or in part in any form.

ALADDIN and related logo are registered trademarks of Simon & Schuster, Inc.

For information about special discounts for bulk purchases,

please contact Simon & Schuster Special Sales at 1-866-506-1949

or business@simonandschuster.com.

The Simon & Schuster Speakers Bureau can bring authors to your live event.

For more information or to book an event contact the

Simon & Schuster Speakers Bureau at 1-866-248-3049

or visit our website at www.simonspeakers.com.

Series designed by Karin Paprocki

Cover designed by Karina Granda

The text of this book was set in Belucian Book.

Manufactured in the United States of America 0119 OFF

4 6 8 10 9 7 5

Library of Congress Control Number 2016954655

ISBN 978-1-4814-4085-1 (hc)

ISBN 978-1-4814-4084-4 (pbk)

ISBN 978-1-4814-4086-8 (eBook)

For Amy Cloud and her fiancé,

Greg Hoffman, best wishes

for much happiness

★ ★ ★ ★

Acknowledgments

To my niece Amanda, who was my flower girl, and to her lovely daughter, Blakely, who will make a beautiful flower girl someday.

Cast of Characters

Shelly

Echo

Kiki

Pearl

Rocky

Contents

Flower Girl Dreams

1

Splash-a-riffic

ISN'T THAT THE MOST FIN-TASTIC purse ever?" Pearl Swamp squealed. She pointed to the cover of a *Mer-Style* magazine with her gold tail fin.

Her best friend, Wanda Slug, moved closer to see the adorable scotch bonnet

★ 1 ★

shell purse. "Ooh, I'm going to ask for one of those for my birthday!" Wanda exclaimed. "I wonder if it comes in pink?"

"Hey, watch out!" Pearl snapped as another third-grade student bumped into her, causing her to drop the magazine.

"Sorry, but I can't be late to class again," Rocky Ridge said. "Or Mrs. Karp will make me shark bait!"

Pearl shook her head and watched Rocky zoom across the huge entrance hall of their school, Trident Academy. He zipped between some chatting sixth graders and a group of fourth graders tossing a puffer-fish ball. It was still a few minutes before school started, and it was unusual for Rocky to hurry to class.

"That Rocky is so rude sometimes," Wanda said, scooping up the magazine and handing it to Pearl. "But he's kind of cute, too."

Pearl giggled. As she turned back to *MerStyle*, she overheard something that made her tail spin. She swirled around to listen to a group of mergirls from her class.

"I can't believe the wedding is in less than one week!" Kiki Coral squealed.

"Who's getting married?" Pearl whispered to Wanda.

Wanda shrugged. "I don't know, but weddings are wave-tastic! I was a flower girl in my cousin Detrella's wedding, and it was a splash."

Pearl sighed. She had always wanted to be a flower girl, ever since she'd attended her own cousin's wedding when she was a small fry. But so far, no one had asked her.

"Let's check with Kiki," Wanda told Pearl. "Maybe the bride is someone we know!"

Wanda swam up to Kiki and said, "We heard you talking about a wedding. Who in the great wide ocean is getting married?"

Pearl couldn't believe Kiki's answer!

2

Mr. Fangtooth's Surprise

MR. FANGTOOTH, THEIR school's grumpy cafeteria worker, was the last merperson in the ocean that Pearl expected to be getting married. Even though he had once saved Pearl from a great white shark, he was still the biggest grouch in Trident City.

After the conch bell sounded to start the school day, Pearl sat at her desk and thought, *Who would want to live the rest of their merlife with a cranky old merman?*

Before class began, Kiki had told Pearl that she, Echo, and their friend Shelly were going to be flower girls in Mr. Fangtooth's wedding. They would get to float down the aisle before the bride, carrying big bunches of flowers. They would probably wear beautiful gowns, too, and maybe even flower crowns. It wasn't fair that they were going to be in a wedding and Pearl was not!

"Today," Mrs. Karp told her third-grade class, "we will begin studying coral reefs.

★ 7 ★

Tomorrow we will go on a short ocean trip to investigate the reef here in Trident City."

"Totally wavy!" Echo said.

Pearl smiled. School was okay, but it was a lot more fun to learn away from her desk. And she did like coral, especially the red coral that grew near the front door of her shell.

"There are both soft and hard corals," Mrs. Karp said. "Who can name a type of hard coral?"

Kiki raised her hand and said, "Brain coral?" She blew her nose into a kelp tissue.

"Very good," Mrs. Karp said. "Are you feeling all right, Kiki?"

Kiki nodded. "I'm allergic to paddle weed, which is blooming right now."

Pearl noticed Kiki's red nose. If Kiki was allergic to flowers, she definitely shouldn't be a flower girl.

There had to be a way for Pearl to be in Mr. Fangtooth's wedding too. After all, she was an expert on sea flowers. And she read every issue of *MerStyle* magazine from start to finish, especially the wedding articles. Plus, Pearl knew how to float with style.

Pearl smiled and made up her mind. She was going to figure out a way to be a flower girl in that wedding, if it was the last thing she did!

How to Be Nice

BY LUNCHTIME, PEARL HAD come up with a plan. If she was really nice to Mr. Fangtooth, he would surely ask her to be a flower girl in his wedding.

But Pearl had never been friendly to Mr. Fangtooth before. She *had* thanked him when he saved her from a shark in Trident Academy's dorm, but otherwise she tried to stay far away from him. After all, who wants to be around a grouch?

Pearl remembered that earlier in the school year Kiki, Shelly, and Echo had tried to make Mr. Fangtooth laugh with funny faces, but it had never worked. So Pearl wasn't exactly sure how to put her plan into action. After all, it was hard to be pleasant to someone who never smiled.

That was it! She would smile at him. As Mr. Fangtooth dished her favorite meal of black-lip oyster and sablefish stew into her shell bowl, Pearl flashed him a huge grin.

★ 12 ★

Mr. Fangtooth looked startled. He frowned even more deeply. "Is something wrong with the food?" he asked.

"No," Pearl said. She showed all her teeth in the biggest smile she could muster.

"Then stop looking at me that way," Mr. Fangtooth grumbled. "You're giving me a headache."

Pearl's smile disappeared. "Well, of all the mean things to say!" she snapped, then slammed her mouth shut. She was trying to make him like her, and fussing wouldn't help.

Pearl sat down at her table and watched Mr. Fangtooth. He frowned at every merstudent in the food line . . . except for Echo. He actually *smiled* at Echo! What had Echo done to make him stop scowling? Pearl had to find out!

As soon as Echo sat down at her corner table with Shelly and Kiki, Pearl rushed over to her. "What in the ocean did you say to Mr. Fangtooth to make him smile?"

Echo, Shelly, and Kiki stared at Pearl blankly.

"I want to make Mr. Fangtooth happy," Pearl explained. "He's such a grouch." She didn't mention that she was doing it so that she could be a flower girl in his wedding.

"That's nice of you," Shelly said. "We used to do the same thing, but it never really worked."

"I just act like I'm glad to see him," Echo suggested. "You could try that."

★ 14 ★

But Pearl's mind stopped on the word "act." Acting! Of course! Pearl had played the part of the sea witch in their third-grade play, *The Little Human*. She had been the star of the show ... sort of. Acting made Pearl happy, but so did singing. Maybe acting *and* singing for Mr. Fangtooth would make him grin.

Pearl glided over to the lunch line, where Mr. Fangtooth was serving other merstudents. She danced in front of the other merkids, acting like a mer-rock star. The whole time she sang a song called "Barracuda" in a squeaky voice.

Pearl knew Mr. Fangtooth would smile. And it might have worked, except she decided to try for a showstopping finish.

She performed a flip called a Scale Dropper. As she spun around, Pearl's tail fin brushed against the edge of a juice stand. A bowl of green seaweed juice sailed through the water and landed with a *splat* right on Mr. Fangtooth's bald head.

"Oh no!" Pearl cried.

Mervelous MerLindas'

PEARL TWISTED HER PEARL
necklace around her hand as
she floated through the door of
her shell home. Usually just touching the
necklace made her feel better, but today it

only reminded her that she wouldn't get to wear it in Mr. Fangtooth's wedding.

"I've been waiting for you, Angelfish!" her mother said as soon as Pearl swam through the entrance. "What took you so long to get home?"

Pearl shrugged. She didn't want to tell her mother that she'd had to stay after school to scrub seaweed juice off the cafeteria floor.

Luckily, her mother didn't give her the chance. "No matter," Mrs. Swamp said. "I'm glad you're here. I just read in the *Trident City Tide* that MerLinda's is having a huge sale. Let's go!"

Pearl barely had time to drop her school bag before her mother whisked her out the door. Clothes shopping at her favorite store in Trident City was usually great fun, but Pearl was still thinking about Mr. Fangtooth's wedding. As they swam closer to MerLinda's, Pearl began to cheer up. Maybe an afternoon of shopping would make her forget about being a flower girl.

Once they arrived, Pearl and her mother browsed racks of beautiful silk dresses and displays of shell jewelry. Then Pearl noticed Shelly, Echo, and Kiki standing in front of a mirror. Each of them wore a matching pale-pink dress.

"Oh, how sweet you mergirls look!" Mrs. Swamp cooed when she saw them. "Is someone you know getting married?"

"We are going to be flower girls in Mr. Fangtooth's wedding. He works at our school," Kiki explained to Mrs. Swamp. "His fiancée, Lillian, is trying on her wedding gown now!"

Kiki pointed to a merlady coming out of a fitting room, wearing a long white gown. Pearl recognized her as the librarian from the Trident City Public Library.

"Oh, I must meet the lovely bride!" Mrs. Swamp gushed as she raced over to Lillian.

Pearl's mother introduced herself. "I just wanted to say hello and congratulations! My name is Helena Swamp, of the Swamp family. You may have heard of us!"

Lillian smiled and nodded. "Of course. I've seen you and your daughter at the library."

Lillian reached to shake Mrs. Swamp's hand, but ended up tripping over the hem of her long gown instead. Pearl grabbed Lillian's arm to keep her from falling.

"Gracious me!" Lillian said. "Thank you!"

Pearl noticed that part of Lillian's dress was twisted around her tail fin. "Actually," Pearl said, "let me help you." In a few tail swishes she had arranged Lillian's gown so that it fanned out like a beautiful shell.

"Oh, I do appreciate that, dear!" Lillian said. "I guess I'm not used to floating in such a long dress." She turned to the mirror.

"And there are so many decisions to make while planning a wedding. It's overwhelming! I can't even decide if I should wear a long veil or a short one."

"Definitely a short veil," Pearl blurted. "It would look fin-tastic with your hair. And you should wear dangly earrings." She snatched a lovely pair of long shell earrings from a nearby counter and handed them to Lillian.

Mrs. Swamp and Lillian both looked at Pearl in surprise.

"Thank you," Lillian said as she put on the jewelry. "These look mervelous!"

Mrs. Swamp nodded approvingly. "My Pearl has always had a flair for fashion. So when is the big day?"

"It's this coming Saturday—less than a week away," Lillian replied, shaking her head. "I still haven't selected my flowers. And our caterer is insisting on serving cuttlefish soup, but my fiancé, Mendel, is allergic! We haven't even seen the room for the ceremony yet. Everything is just a mess!"

As Mrs. Swamp and Lillian discussed the wedding, Pearl swam over to Shelly, Kiki, and Echo. Pearl tried to be nice to them, even though *she* wanted to be the one wearing a pink dress.

"You make pretty flower girls," she told them.

Shelly smiled. "Thanks. Being in a wedding is so exciting!"

Echo's dark eyes sparkled. "This is the first wedding I've ever been in."

Pearl's mother hustled over to them. "Pearl, we really should get to shopping. But you did a lovely job arranging Lillian's dress," Mrs. Swamp commented. "And your suggestions for the veil and earrings were perfect. Maybe you should be a wedding planner when you grow up!"

Pearl didn't want to discuss weddings anymore. Seeing the mergirls in their flower girl dresses made her sad. She hated the fact that she was going to miss out on all the wedding fun.

5

Project Flower Girl

THAT NIGHT, WHILE PEARL ate her dinner of milkfish and striped catfish soup, she tried to come up with another way to be in Mr. Fangtooth's wedding.

Then, as she ran her Venus comb

through her hair twenty times before going to bed, she remembered what her mother had said: Pearl would make a great wedding planner when she grew up.

What if she didn't wait until she grew up? Pearl could help plan Lillian's wedding to Mr. Fangtooth right now! After all, Lillian seemed clueless when it came to being a bride. She hadn't even selected her flowers yet. The wedding was Saturday and it was already Tuesday! If Pearl helped with the wedding, then Lillian and Mr. Fangtooth had to see that Pearl would be the perfect flower girl.

Pearl climbed into bed and fell asleep with flower girl dreams in her head.

She woke up the next morning very

early. She could hardly wait to start her new plan: Project Flower Girl.

When she got to school, she remembered that it was the day Mrs. Karp's class was taking an ocean trip to the coral reef. The third graders buzzed with excitement.

"All right, students," Mrs. Karp told them as they lined up at the classroom door. "Please study the reef carefully without touching it. Make a list of all the different types of coral you see. Next week you will each give an oral report sharing information about coral."

At the word "report," Pearl heard a big groan from Rocky. Pearl felt the same way, but she didn't complain. In fact, she was sure that seeing all the beautiful coral would give her even more ideas for Lillian's wedding. Maybe they could use pieces of coral for the table centerpieces at the wedding dinner!

The entire class swam to the reef together. When they arrived, Pearl saw a patch of orange, pink, and green coral and a school of butterfly fish hovering nearby. A bright green polka-dotted parrot fish floated past some branches of bushy black coral. Pearl was wondering whether yellow, flowerlike dendrophyllid coral or daisy coral would look prettier on the tables at Lillian's wedding when she overheard Echo speaking to Wanda.

"That's where Mr. Fangtooth and Lillian are getting married," Echo told Wanda. Echo pointed to the elegant

Trident Plaza Hotel, which was built into the coral reef nearby.

"Ooh," Wanda said. "Is it going to be a fancy wedding?"

Echo shrugged. "Yesterday Lillian said she was thinking about having passion flower feather stars and flower urchins brought in to decorate for the reception.

And she is pretty sure that our bouquets will be golden dune moss tied up with Neptune's necklace."

Pearl swam over to Echo and Wanda. "But that's not right at all!" Pearl blurted. "Everyone knows that sea lavender is all the rage for weddings at this time of year! Golden dune moss is *so* last season. I read all about it in the newest *MerStyle* magazine!"

Echo looked at Pearl in surprise. "But that's what Lillian wants, and she's the bride."

Pearl folded her arms over her chest. "Lillian doesn't know what she's doing. She said so at MerLinda's yesterday." She paused before asking, "Why did Lillian and Mr. Fangtooth ask you, Shelly, and Kiki to be in their wedding, anyway? What makes *you* so special?"

"Pearl!" Wanda said. "That's none of your business. Mr. Fangtooth and Lillian can ask whoever they want."

"It's all right," Echo said before turning to Pearl. "Lillian and Mr. Fangtooth asked us to be in their wedding because Shelly and I found a love letter that Lillian had dropped. Mr. Fangtooth had written it to Lillian very long ago. When we gave it to Mr. Fangtooth, he realized that Lillian still cared for him."

But Pearl wasn't satisfied and asked, "What about Kiki?"

Echo shrugged. "Kiki was with us when we met Lillian."

Pearl sighed. That did explain why Lillian and Mr. Fangtooth had asked Echo, Shelly, and Kiki to be in the wedding, but it still didn't help Pearl.

Pearl tapped her chin. There was no way she could write a love letter. But she could definitely help Lillian. In fact, she knew that unless she helped Lillian, the entire wedding would be a disaster.

And Lillian would be so grateful, Pearl was sure to be a flower girl!

6

Making a List

AFTER SCHOOL, PEARL RACED into her bedroom and spread her *MerStyle* magazines on the floor around her gold tail. She opened each one to the wedding section and began to make a list of the best ideas. Lillian hadn't been lying. There were so many decisions to make! Centerpieces for the dinner tables, flowers, bouquets, favors . . .

"For shark's sake!" Pearl muttered. "I never knew planning a wedding was so much work. I wonder if Lillian has even thought about the music."

Pearl decided that if she was going to be a wedding planner, she'd need a business card. So she made her own out of small pieces of kelp, writing *Pearl Swamp, Trident City's Top Wedding Planner* on each in black octopus ink.

Just then Anna came into the room with a

Pearl Swamp
Trident City's
Top Wedding Planner

stack of clean clothes for Pearl. Anna was the Swamp family's maid, but she was more like a second mom to Pearl. Pearl looked at Anna's wrinkled face and realized she was probably the same age as Lillian.

"Anna?" Pearl asked. "If you were getting married all over again, would you rather carry a bouquet of sea lavender or golden dune moss?" Surely Lillian would like sea lavender better. After all, it was Queen Edwina's favorite flower, and she was royalty!

Anna winked as she put Pearl's clothes on her bed. "Is my little Pearl planning her wedding already?" she asked. "Perhaps you have a crush? The mayor's cute son, Rocky?"

"No!" Pearl sputtered. "Not me! It's for a friend."

Anna smiled like she didn't believe Pearl. "Sure it is!"

"Really," Pearl said as she felt her face turning red. "I *am* helping a friend." Which Pearl didn't think was a lie, because she was helping Mr. Fangtooth in a way, and she had *tried* to be his friend. It wasn't her fault that he didn't like her smile or her singing.

Pearl tried a different question. "What was your favorite part of your wedding?" She knew that Anna had been married for more than thirty years.

Anna's eyes got a faraway look. "The best part was marrying the merman I loved. And having my family and friends all around me."

Pearl nodded, but she didn't believe Anna. Her wedding must not have been very good.

Pearl wanted to make sure that Lillian and Mr. Fangtooth would have wonderful memories of their special day. She couldn't wait to get started!

7

Miss Fix-It

THE NEXT DAY PEARL COULD hardly wait for school to be over. When Mrs. Karp asked Pearl a question about mushroom coral, Pearl had to admit she hadn't been listening.

"Miss Swamp," Mrs. Karp told her. "Please pay attention in class."

"Yes, Mrs. Karp," Pearl answered. And she did try to listen as her teacher talked about the stringlike whip coral, but then she started thinking about how clueless Lillian had been about her wedding. Lillian truly didn't seem to know what she was doing. She needed a lot of help, and Pearl couldn't wait to fix everything for her. So when the conch sounded to end the school day, Pearl blasted out of her seat and soared to the Trident Plaza Hotel.

She didn't even glance at the shining brass walls or the green marble floors of the hotel's lobby. Instead she swam straight to the enormous brass-and-marble check-in desk. A burly merman with a bushy mustache smiled at her and said, "How may I assist you?"

Pearl looked at his name tag and nodded. "Leroy, can you introduce me to the person who takes care of weddings? I am helping Mr. Fangtooth and Lillian plan theirs for this coming Saturday."

"I am in charge of all the weddings at the Plaza," Leroy told her.

"You?" Pearl gasped. For some reason she had expected a merlady to be in charge. She nodded her head and said, "I would like to review all the arrangements right away, please."

Leroy frowned. "This is a most unusual request for someone who isn't the bride or groom, but since we are not busy right now, I would be happy to go over everything with you."

Pearl almost giggled. This was going to be easier than she thought.

"Let's start with the location of the ceremony," Leroy said. He led her into a dark room that smelled like dirty clothes. "It will take place in here."

"No, no, no!" Pearl shouted. "This will never work! Did Lillian and Mr. Fangtooth approve this?"

Leroy shrugged. "They haven't seen it yet."

Pearl crossed her arms. "Well, I'm seeing it now, and this will not do. What else do you have available?"

Pearl and Leroy spent the next hour checking out different rooms before they found one overlooking a waterfall. An enormous golden chandelier glittering with plankton hung from the center of the carved floral ceiling.

"This is perfect!" Pearl said. "We will move the ceremony to this room. Next, we need to go over the chairs, the flowers, the music, and the special white aisle for the bride to float down. And of course, we'll need some sort of lovely flower arbor for Lillian and Mr. Fangtooth to stand under."

Leroy rubbed his forehead. "Is that all?"

"Oh, no," Pearl said with a smile. "We're just getting started."

8

Perfectly Costly

I HAVE A TERRIBLE HEADACHE," Leroy said. Pearl had just insisted on shell baskets of sea lavender accented with pearls for the centerpieces. She'd been upset when Leroy told her the hotel's policy on not using live coral, but the sea lavender would be even prettier. "Are we finished?"

Pearl looked at her list and nodded. Everything was crossed off. Lillian and Mr. Fangtooth were going to be so happy when they saw all that Pearl had done. Of course they would want her to be one of their flower girls!

"All right," Leroy said, holding up his own list of all the changes Pearl had made. "Let me calculate how much this is going to cost."

Cost? Pearl hadn't thought about the price. She looked at Leroy's list. It was very long. Pearl hoped all her suggestions wouldn't be too expensive. Her parents bought her everything she needed, but they gave her a small allowance. Pearl had a few shells saved for a new purse, so she could use those to help with the extra wedding cost if it wasn't too much.

Pearl looked around the beautiful room she'd chosen. It was so much better than that stinky dark place. Surely Lillian and Mr. Fangtooth would rather be here, no matter how expensive it might be. With a sigh she followed Leroy back to the check-in desk.

Pearl watched Leroy as he added numbers together. Then he added more numbers together. He shook his head and added even more numbers. Finally, after what seemed like forever, Leroy lifted his head and smiled. Only he wasn't smiling at Pearl.

Pearl turned around and was shocked to see Lillian standing behind her.

"Welcome!" Leroy greeted her. "I have wonderful news. Even though it's only a few days away, we can easily make all the changes that you want for your wedding."

"What changes?" Lillian asked, fanning herself with her tail.

Pearl patted Lillian on the shoulder. "Hello! Remember me from MerLinda's? I'm Pearl Swamp, wedding planner." She reached into her shell purse and handed Lillian a business card. "I noticed how stressed out you were, so I fixed everything. Don't worry, your wedding will be beautiful!"

"And it will only cost ten thousand more shells," Leroy added.

Pearl gulped. "Did you say ten thousand?" That was a lot more than she had in her savings.

Lillian gasped. "But—but I don't have ten thousand shells."

"What about Mr. Fangtooth?" Pearl asked. "I'm sure he wants to pay for a nice wedding."

Lillian shook her head. "But we decided to split the costs. I am paying for the wedding and Mendel is paying for the honeymoon. Oh, Pearl, what have you done?"

9

Wedding Planner Woes

NOW PEARL HAD A TERRIBLE headache!

Leroy led Pearl and Lillian back into the beautiful room Pearl had picked for the ceremony. Lillian looked at Leroy's list and shook her head. "All of this sounds lovely, but I just can't afford it."

Pearl smiled. "You mean . . . you like my ideas?"

Lillian sighed. "Of course! Just look at this," she said, glancing around the beautiful space. "Your list, this room . . . it's as if all my wishes have come true."

As she spoke, Lillian had a dreamy, happy look on her face. Even though Pearl hardly knew Lillian, suddenly she wanted the librarian to have the perfect wedding. Even if Pearl *wasn't* a flower girl.

But where could she get that many shells? There had to be a way! "Don't worry about the added cost," Pearl said, trying to sound confident. "I am going to make sure you don't have to pay extra."

"You are?" Lillian and Leroy said together.

"Of course," Pearl said. "After all, I *am* a wedding planner. Just leave it all to me!"

Lillian shook her head. "That's sweet of you, dear, but I think we'd better just put things back the way they were."

Pearl couldn't stand the idea of Lillian getting married in that dark, dank room with the wrong kind of flowers and no centerpieces. "Could you give me just one day to fix things? Please!"

"All right," Lillian finally agreed. "But I don't see how it will work."

Pearl didn't either, but she wasn't going to tell Lillian or Leroy that. Instead, she twisted her necklace and started thinking.

She thought during her swim home. She thought when she should have been doing her homework.

She was still thinking at the dinner table.

"Pearl, stop playing with your coconut crab legs and eat your dinner," her mother told her.

Pearl gazed at the portrait of her mother and father on their wedding day. Her aunt Joan had sketched it, and it had hung in their dining room for as long as Pearl could remember. Why hadn't she thought of asking her mother and father for their advice?

"Mom, did you and Daddy spend a lot of shells on your wedding?" Pearl asked them.

Mr. Swamp laughed, almost spitting out his comb jelly tea. "No! We got married on the budget plan."

"Budget?" Pearl asked.

Mrs. Swamp frowned at her husband. "What your father means," she said, "is that we had to be creative and make a lot out of a little. We needed all our shells just to live back then."

"So how were you creative?"

"Well," Mrs. Swamp said, "it was a long time ago, but I remember feeling lucky that your grandfather was in the Shark Patrol. We got lots of discounts because of that."

"Grandpa Swamp was in the Shark
Patrol?" Pearl asked. The Shark Patrol
protected merfolk from sharks and any

other dangers in Trident City. And Pearl knew that Mr. Fangtooth was a retired colonel from the Shark Patrol.

"No, *my* father. Your grandfather Whipray," Mrs. Swamp said. "Because the merfolk of Trident City appreciated his hard work protecting us from sharks, they gave him discounts on plenty of things—food, manta ray trips, and even his shell home."

"Didn't you and your sisters make the decorations for our tables, too?" Mr. Swamp asked his wife. "They were very pretty."

Mrs. Swamp smiled at her husband. "And I loved how you put starfish all over the room."

Suddenly Pearl's head no longer hurt. She was forming a plan, but there wasn't much time to get everything together before the wedding.

Pearl crossed her tail fins and hoped her plan wouldn't be a total disaster!

10

Pearl's Plan

THE NEXT MORNING PEARL arrived at school extra early. She swam back and forth in the front hall of Trident Academy. She didn't even bother to look at the colorful carvings that filled the high ceiling. "Where are Kiki, Shelly, and Echo?" she muttered to herself.

"Hi, Pearl," Wanda said, floating up to her. "What are you doing here so early?"

Pearl grinned and hugged Wanda. "I have a fin-tastic idea. Will you help me?"

Wanda shrugged. "Of course! But what's your idea?"

Luckily, just then Pearl spotted Echo and Shelly chatting with Kiki on the other side of the enormous hall. "Come on," Pearl said, pulling Wanda along. "We need their help too."

"Hi, Wanda! Hi, Pearl. What's up?" Shelly asked.

"What's up is that Lillian's wedding is going to be a total flop unless we all work together to save it," Pearl told them.

"What are you talking about?" Kiki said.

Echo put her hands on her hips. "Pearl! Are you just saying that because you want to take over?"

"No. And I don't care about being a flower girl anymore either," Pearl said, which wasn't exactly true. Of course she'd love to be a flower girl, but now she realized that some things were more important— like making Lillian happy. "Listen to this."

Pearl went on to describe the horrible dark room where Lillian was going to have her wedding, as well as all the beautiful things that Lillian couldn't afford.

"But with the Shark Patrol discount— and if we make the centerpieces and flower arrangements ourselves—we can still make at least some of Lillian's dreams come true," Pearl said. She kept her tail fins crossed, hoping the mergirls would want to help. There was no way she could do it by herself.

"My mom works at the Conservatory for the Preservation of Sea Horses and Swordfish, which is inside the hotel. She might be able to convince them to donate the room for the ceremony," Echo suggested.

"Grandfather Siren might have some things in his storage closets that we can use for decorations," Shelly said. Shelly's grandfather ran Trident City's People Museum

and was known for having unusual objects for the mergirls to borrow for school projects.

"Shelly, since you have such a pretty voice, could you sing at the wedding?" Pearl asked.

Shelly's face turned red, but she nodded. "Sure."

"I'll do whatever I can," Kiki said. "My grandmother taught me how to arrange flowers. Of course, we never use paddle weed, since I'm allergic to that."

"We'll all help," Wanda agreed. "This is so exciting! There's only one problem. . . ."

11

Dr. Bottom's Gift

SCHOOL WAS THE PROBLEM! Pearl and the mergirls wanted to get started on their wedding ideas, but instead they had to sit in class and listen to Mrs. Karp discuss creatures that live near coral reefs. Pearl was deep in thought when Wanda poked her tail.

"Look at those," Wanda whispered. "Wouldn't they make perfect centerpieces for the tables?"

Mrs. Karp held up what looked like a delicate white flower vase. "This is a reef-forming sponge. Dr. Bottom was kind enough to donate one for each of you to study." Dr. Bottom was Trident's Academy's fourth-grade teacher, but he often taught Mrs. Karp's third graders science. "While not coral, they are similar in some ways."

Pearl's hand shot up in the water. "Mrs. Karp, I have a very important question to ask the class. It's about someone who works at Trident Academy, so it's related to school."

Mrs. Karp sighed. "What is it, Pearl?"

"Could we borrow every student's reef-forming sponge for Mr. Fangtooth's wedding? We'd give them back right afterward."

Mrs. Karp raised a green eyebrow before saying, "Let's take a vote. Raise your hand if you are okay with Pearl borrowing your sponge."

Everyone raised their hand except Rocky. Pearl, Echo, Shelly, and Kiki glared at him until he raised his hand too.

"Thank you! That will be a big help,"

Pearl said. "Now, we just need to get some sea flowers to fill them."

Rocky shook his head. "I think jewel anemones would be much prettier. There are a whole bunch floating beside Zollie's corral. You could use those." Zollie was Rocky's sea horse.

Pearl couldn't believe that Rocky was being so nice. "Thanks," she told him.

"May I also suggest some pink lace bryozoan?" Mrs. Karp added. "I have been saving some for a special occasion, and I'd love to help Mr. Fangtooth."

"Mervelous! Thanks, Mrs. Karp," Pearl said,

and she meant it. School hadn't been a problem after all. In fact, being in class had actually *helped* them with the wedding!

"Let's work on the centerpieces and everything else after school," Echo whispered as Mrs. Karp continued the lesson.

Pearl smiled. "We can meet at the Trident City Plaza. I'm going to explain everything to Leroy and beg him to give Lillian a discount." Pearl hoped that the fact that Mr. Fangtooth was in the Shark Patrol would be enough to give Lillian and Mr. Fangtooth a wonderful wedding on a budget.

Genius

PEARL COULDN'T BELIEVE the scene awaiting her at the Trident Plaza Hotel after school. Instead of four mergirls, it looked like half of Trident City had turned up to help with the wedding.

Echo floated up to Pearl. "I hope you don't mind," Echo said. "I told a few merfolk about decorating today, and they all wanted to help."

Pearl raised an eyebrow. "A few merfolk?"

Echo shrugged. "The word must have spread. Are you mad?"

"Are you kidding?" Pearl asked. "This is shelltacular!"

When Leroy saw the large group of Shark Patrol guards, librarians, and Trident Academy teachers in the lobby, he agreed to give Lillian and Mr. Fangtooth a huge discount on the cost of food. Echo's mother convinced the president of the Conservatory for the Preservation of

Sea Horses and Swordfish to donate the beautiful room for the ceremony.

Mrs. Karp arrived with an armful of pink lace bryozoan. Rocky rode in on Zollie, carrying kelp bags full of jewel anemones.

"Look what we found in MerPark," Kiki said, showing Pearl a huge bouquet of deep green mermaid's wineglass. Shelly followed her, holding feathery white sea lilies.

"Those will be so pretty for Lillian and her bridesmaids and flower girls," Pearl said with a nod. "I think they are even more elegant than sea lavender."

She felt a little pang of sadness that she wouldn't be one of the flower girls, but she took a deep breath and brushed those feelings aside. There wasn't time to worry about it!

"Let's get busy!" Pearl said.

And they did. By the time they were finished, the Shark Patrol guards and librarians had made a fabulous arbor covered with flowers. The Trident Academy teachers decorated the aisle leading up to the arbor with pink lace bryozoan. Pearl and her merfriends had made lovely arrangements using the reef-forming sponges, sea anemones, and some fake human pearls that Shelly's grandfather had donated for the event.

"It's all so pretty," Wanda said. "I wish we had one of those human objects that could take a picture."

"A picture! Of course!" Pearl shrieked. "Wanda, you're a genius!" She had forgotten all about her parents' wedding portrait. She needed to make sure Lillian and Mr. Fangtooth had a picture to remember their wedding day too.

Pearl floated over to where the Trident Academy teachers were placing some flowers around the shell chairs. "Miss Haniver, would you mind drawing a portrait of Mr. and Mrs. Fangtooth on their wedding day?" she asked the art teacher.

Miss Haniver smiled. "I would be delighted! It will be my gift to them."

"Wonderful!" Pearl said. She looked around the room at all the merpeople who were working so hard to make it a special day for Lillian and Mr. Fangtooth. She couldn't wait to swim over to the library to tell Lillian everything they had done.

But Pearl didn't need to go anywhere.

"What in the ocean is going on here?" a voice said. Pearl whirled around to find Lillian and Mr. Fangtooth floating in the doorway.

Help!

"COME ALONG, PEARL," Mrs. Swamp said the next morning. The two were on their way to a Saturday brunch at the Coral Table restaurant at the Trident Plaza Hotel. "Why are you being so slow?"

Pearl dragged her tail in the sand. It was the day of Mr. Fangtooth and Lillian's wedding, and she had been sad since the moment she'd opened her eyes. Even if Pearl couldn't be a flower girl, she still would have liked to have been there.

Mr. Fangtooth and Lillian had been thrilled with how everything looked. They thanked everyone—especially Pearl—for all their hard work. Pearl was proud to have made their wedding so special.

When they finally reached the paved plaza in front of the hotel, Pearl saw Lillian swimming out the door in her beautiful wedding dress. It was almost time for the wedding ceremony to begin! Why was Lillian *leaving* the hotel?

"There you are!" Lillian said, her veil floating in the water around her. "I was just about to swim to your shell!"

"Is something wrong?" Pearl asked

Lillian looked Pearl up and down. "Yes, in fact something *is* wrong. Can you do me a big favor?"

Pearl nodded. "Of course."

"Come with me," Lillian said, grabbing Pearl's hand and pulling her through the hotel lobby.

"What's happening?" Pearl's mother asked, floating behind them.

Lillian took Pearl into a lavishly decorated dressing room. Pearl was surprised to see several older mermaids, along with

Echo and Shelly, floating there. They were all dressed in the same lovely shade of pink.

Echo swam up to Pearl. "Thank goodness you're here! Did you come to save the day?"

Before Pearl could answer, her mother spoke up. "We were just going to eat brunch when Lillian grabbed Pearl," Mrs. Swamp said, her hands on her hips. "Would someone please tell me what's going on?"

"We have a bit of a crisis on our fins," Lillian said. "Kiki's allergies got much worse and—"

"Oh no!" Pearl interrupted. "But we were so careful not to use paddle weed in the bouquets."

"She found out she's allergic to mermaid's wineglass too," Lillian said.

Echo nodded. "She's all swollen and her arms are itching like crazy."

"Dr. Weedly told her to rest so she'll be better tomorrow. The trouble is," Lillian continued, "we are short one flower girl."

She grabbed Pearl's shoulders. "Pearl, will you help us? Will you be my flower girl?"

Pearl's eyes grew wide. Was Lillian serious?

The Wedding

"OH, PUPFISH, YOU LOOK beautiful," Pearl's mother whispered in her ear. Pearl smiled, but inside she felt scared!

Why was she afraid? She'd always wanted to be a flower girl. Now she was wearing a pale-pink dress that matched Shelly's and Echo's. In her hands she held a bouquet of sea lilies and mermaid's wineglass.

Pearl stared into the dressing-room mirror. Her hair was swept up in a lovely swirl with jewel anemones pinned to it. She had never looked more elegant, yet she was nervous. Everyone had worked so hard to make things perfect. What if Pearl ruined the wedding? What if she tripped and fell floating down the aisle? Lillian would never forgive her!

"Time to take your places," Lillian told Pearl, Echo, and Shelly. "Pearl, just follow your friends and float down the aisle."

Pearl must have looked as terrified as she felt, because Lillian leaned down and whispered, "Oh, little shell, are you all right?"

Pearl didn't want to ruin Lillian's dream wedding, but she couldn't help blurting, "I don't want to make a mistake."

Lillian gave Pearl a serious look before laughing. "Oh, Pearl, I'm not one of those crazy brides who gets her tail in a knot if everything isn't perfect."

"You're not?" Pearl asked.

"No! In fact, if something goes wrong, it will give us something to laugh about later," Lillian said. "The important thing is that Mendel and I are getting married.

The only thing you have to worry about is having a mervelous time."

Pearl smiled at Lillian. "I can do that," she said.

Pearl slowly swam into the lovely ceremony room. She followed Echo and Shelly as they glided under the upturned swords of an entire Shark Patrol squadron. Mr. Fangtooth floated at the end of the aisle lined with flower urchins and pink lace bryozoan. He stood with Reverend Finley under an archway covered with passion flower feather stars. Mr. Fangtooth looked nervous as Pearl took her place at the front of the room. But when Lillian floated into the room in her beautiful wedding dress,

Mr. Fangtooth's face lit up in the biggest smile ever.

That's when Pearl realized that weddings weren't about flower girls, or fancy flowers, or even about pretty dresses. Weddings were about two people who really cared for

each other, who wanted to spend their lives together. And they didn't need a flower girl to do that!

But still, Pearl couldn't help grinning from ear to ear. Finally her flower girl dreams had come true!

Class
Reports

SHELLY SIREN

"Hi, I'm Shelly Siren. I'm pretending to be reporting live from a fringing reef. What is a fringing reef, you might ask? Well, I can tell you because my friend Lillian showed me a book about reefs at the Trident City Public Library. A fringing reef is a reef right next to a piece of land with no deep water in between."

ECHO REEF

"Hello, I'm Echo Reef. My name is the same as some of the most beautiful eco-systems in the ocean. There are two main kinds of coral: warm and cold. The cold-water coral reefs are in deeper water. The three main types of reefs are fringing, barrier, and atoll."

ROCKY RIDGE

"Rocky Ridge here at the site of the Great Barrier Reef. It's the ocean's largest reef. I'm seeing every color of soft coral here. Did you know that a barrier reef is separated from land by a lagoon? That means that the reef isn't right up beside the land."

PEARL SWAMP

"I am Pearl Swamp, reporting on an atoll. It's a ring of coral around a body of water. I've never actually seen one, but Kiki told me about one called the Aldabra Atoll, which sticks up out of the water and looks like a huge mushroom rock."

KIKI CORAL

"Since my last name is Coral, I am very interested in coral reefs. Did you know that many reefs are in serious danger? Never buy or wear jewelry made from living coral. And did you know one touch of your hand can kill live coral? Some humans use a poison called sodium cyanide to catch reef fish! The fish are all right after a while, but the poison kills coral."

The Mermaid Song Tales

REFRAIN:

Let the water roar

Deep down we're swimming along

Twirling, swirling, singing the mermaid song.

VERSE 1:

Shelly flips her tail

Racing, diving, chasing a whale

Twirling, swirling, singing the mermaid song.

★ 94 ★

VERSE 2:

Pearl likes to shine

Oh my Neptune, she looks so fine

Twirling, swirling, singing the mermaid song.

VERSE 3:

Shining Echo flips her tail

Backward and forward without fail

Twirling, swirling, singing the mermaid song.

VERSE 4:

Amazing Kiki

Far from home and floating so free

Twirling, swirling, singing the mermaid song.

Author's Note

THIS YEAR I WILL CELEBRATE my thirty-fourth wedding anniversary, but I remember my wedding like it happened yesterday. Since blue is my favorite color, I had white roses with blue ribbons in all the bouquets. I had a long white gown with a lacy white veil. Eric, my husband-to-be, wore a gray tux with a white rose boutonniere. He was even more nervous than Mr. Fangtooth!

I had one flower girl, my niece Amanda,
who wore a blue dress with lots of ruffles.
She was prettier than a mermaid!

Your mermaid friend,

Debbie Dadey

Glossary

ANGELFISH: The queen angelfish is one of the most colorful of the Caribbean reef fish. Adults are blue and yellow.

BARRACUDA: The fast-moving barracuda has needle-sharp teeth and a long body.

BLACK-LIP OYSTER: This oyster lives in many parts of the world, including the Gulf of Mexico.

BUSHY BLACK CORAL: This coral has branches that look like large bird feathers.

BUTTERFLYFISH: If a coral reef is healthy, it will have lots of bright yellow butterfly-fish. You can identify them by their blue eye patch.

COCONUT CRAB: Robber crab is another name for this arthropod. It lives on the land, but lays eggs in the water.

COMB JELLY: The comb jelly causes a lot of trouble in the Black Sea by eating fish eggs.

CONCH: Conch are mollusks with a lovely spiral shell. In the past, jewelry was made out of the shell.

CUTTLEFISH: The cuttlefish can darken its entire body when it passes over some-thing dark.

DAISY CORAL: This coral looks surpris-ingly like a daisy flower.

DENDROPHYLLID CORAL: Usually during the day this coral is a red lump, but when darkness falls, it makes a spectacular orange-and-yellow flowerlike display.

FLOWER URCHIN: This creature has flowerlike appendages, but watch out—it is very poisonous!

GOLDEN DUNE MOSS: This moss grows on sand dunes and gives the sand a golden color.

JEWEL ANEMONE: Jewel anemones can be any color and often cover underwater cliffs with their flowerlike disks.

KELP: Giant kelp is the largest of all seaweed.

MERMAID'S WINEGLASS: This little green algae grows along the coast, so someone must have dropped it in MerPark in order for Kiki to find it.

MILKFISH: This silver fish has a forked tail. It is important for food in parts of Asia.

MUSHROOM CORAL: Most corals live in groups, but the mushroom coral lives as an individual. Its skeleton is shaped like a mushroom.

NEPTUNE'S NECKLACE: This brown seaweed resembles a string of beads.

PADDLE WEED: This sea grass is the favorite food of the dugong, a creature that looks similar to a manatee.

PARROT FISH: In Polynesia, parrot fish is served raw and was once only eaten by the king.

PASSION FLOWER FEATHER STAR: This feather star has eighteen to twenty arms of different lengths, giving it a flowerlike look.

PEARLS: An oyster forms a pearl when a tiny piece of sand gets inside its shell. The oyster coats the sand with a shiny substance to make a lovely pearl that is often used in jewelry.

PINK LACE BRYOZOAN: A colony, or group, of these creatures looks like a bunch of pink potato chips clustered together.

PLANKTON: Plankton are small creatures that drift on the surface of the water.

PUFFER FISH: The skin and some parts of a star puffer fish are very poisonous, but in Japan it is considered a delicacy.

Only specially trained chefs are permitted to prepare it, since they know the parts that are safe to eat.

RED CORAL: The deep-red Mediterranean coral has been collected for centuries to be made into jewelry and is now scarce. It is also called precious coral.

REEF-FORMING SPONGE: This sponge looks very much like a pretty white vase to put flowers in.

SABLEFISH: Sablefish do not reproduce very quickly. In fact, it takes fourteen years to replace one.

SCOTCH BONNET: The shell of this sea snail resembles a woolen cap (or Scotch bonnet) that was once worn in Scotland, giving this lovely shell its name.

SEA HORSE: This tiny ocean creature resembles a horse but is a terrible swimmer.

SEA LAVENDER: This plant, often called statice, grows near the coast and has showy light-purple flowers.

SEA LILY: This white relative of the feather star lives in deep water.

SEAWEED: There are many types of seaweed. Seaweed does not have roots, but floats freely in water.

SHARK: Sharks are often thought of as the ocean's bad guys (especially the great white shark), but they are actually needed to keep the fish population healthy and strong.

STARFISH: More correctly called a sea star, this creature usually has five arms.

STRIPED CATFISH: This striped fish lives in coral reefs. A sting from an adult is very dangerous to humans.

SWORDFISH: This creature gets its name from its long, swordlike bill. It is also known as a broadbill.

VENUS COMB: This snail has long, thin spines that would work well as a mermaid's comb.

WHIP CORAL: Whip coral is also known as wire coral because it grows in a single branch that is sometimes coiled.

Debbie Dadey

is the author and coauthor of more than
one hundred and sixty children's books,
including the series The Adventures of
the Bailey School Kids. A former teacher
and librarian, Debbie and her family live
in Sevierville, Tennessee. She hopes you'll
visit www.debbiedadey.com for lots of mermaid fun.

Mermaid Tales

Can't get enough of the
Trident Academy merkids?
Visit MermaidTalesBooks.com
for activities, excerpts, and more!

ALADDIN

Looking for another great book?
Find it
IN THE MIDDLE.

Fun, fantastic books for kids
in the in-be**TWEEN** age.

IntheMiddleBooks.com

Join Willa and the Chincoteague ponies on their island adventures!

SEP 2019

Sparkle Spa

Making friends one Sparkly nail at a time!

All That Glitters

Purple Nails and Puppy Tails

Makeover Magic

True Colors

Bad News Nails

A Picture-Perfect Mess

Bling It On!

EBOOK EDITIONS ALSO AVAILABLE

From Aladdin • KIDS.SimonandSchuster.com